Scribble

Ruth Ohi

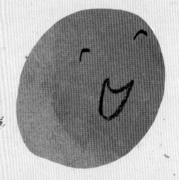

North Winds Press
An Imprint of Scholastic Canada Ltd.

To Kaarel.
— Ruth

The artwork was rendered primarily in watercolour, pencil crayon, pastel and found paper, then assembled digitally.

Library and Archives Canada Cataloguing in Publication
Ohi, Ruth, author, illustrator
Scribble / Ruth Ohi.
ISBN 978-1-4431-4665-4 (bound)
I. Title.
PS8579.H47S37 2016   jC813'.6   C2015-905472-9

www.scholastic.ca

Author photo by Annie T.

6 5 4 3 2 1   Printed in Malaysia 108   16 17 18 19 20

I like to roll, around and around!

I like to sit still.
I am solid and strong.

I have many points — all of
them good ones.

Straight lines are best.

Wa-hooo!

Follow me and you will
never get lost!

Za-Zoom!

Swish!

"Eek!" said Circle.

"Ack!" said Square.

Triangle trembled.

"What are you?" said Circle.

"I am Scribble," said Scribble.

"That is not a shape," said Square.

"Too many points," said Triangle.

"Do you want to play?"
said Scribble.

"With you?" said Square.

"Together?" said Triangle.

"But why?" said Circle.

So Scribble swooped.

And Circle found out
that when scribbles waved . . .

. . . circles shone bright.

When scribbles scurried,
circles could bounce up . . .

. . . and down.

When Circle feared
she would float away,

Scribble held on tight.

When Scribble roared,

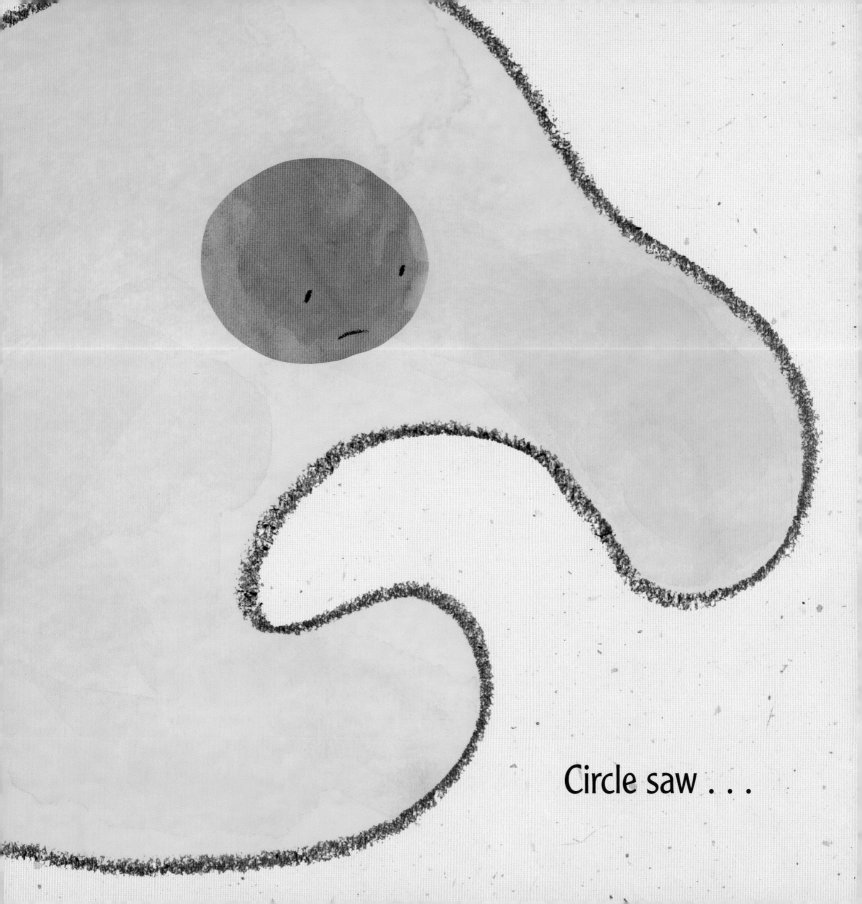

Circle saw . . .

And Circle saw Square and
Triangle wanting to join in.

"Come," said Circle. "Come play."

"Come, see what else you can be!"

"Hello. My name is Star!"